# THE OFFICIAL
# BIRMINGHAM CITY
# FOOTBALL CLUB
# ANNUAL 2025

**Written by Andy Greeves**
**Designed by Jon Dalrymple**
**Contributions by Cathryn Greeves**

A Grange Publication

ISBN 978-1-915879-77-6

# CONTENTS

# WELCOME

## Welcome to the 2025 Official Birmingham City Annual

2025 is a special year for Birmingham City FC as the Club celebrates its 150th anniversary.

This Annual begins with a look back through 150 years of Blues history, from their foundation as Small Heath Alliance back in 1875 through to the current day.

Elsewhere in this Annual, we profile the players who represent Chris Davies' Men's and Amy Merricks' Women's squads. We have an exclusive interview with lifelong Blues fan and UB40 drummer Jimmy Brown, who talks football and music, while there is a crossword, wordsearch and Blues Super Quiz, to test your knowledge of the Club.

There is also a look back at the 2023/24 season at St. Andrew's @ Knighthead Park with reviews of the campaign for Blues' Men's and Women's teams.

Happy 150th birthday Birmingham City Football Club!

Enjoy your new Annual and Keep Right On!

#Blues #BCFC #KRO

Andy Greeves

# MY BLUES ANNUAL

My name is: _____

and I am a Birmingham City Supporter!

Here is a picture of me:

I am _____ years old

I was born in _____ on ____ /____ /_____

I live in _____

Make this Annual your own record of your time as a Blues supporter.
Fill in all the details about yourself (don't forget your photo),
your first Blues match and pick your very own dream team!

**My three favourite current Blues players are:**

1. _____

2. _____

3. _____

**My first Blues match was against**

_____

**The full-time result was BIRMINGHAM CITY** _____

_____

**I play football for a team called**

_____

**My best starting XI for Birmingham City for the 2024/25 season would be:**

GK – _____

RB – _____

CB – _____

CB – _____

LB – _____

RM – _____

CM – _____

CM – _____

LM – _____

FW – _____

FW – _____

# 150 YEARS OF BIRMINGHAM CITY FOOTBALL CLUB

## AS BLUES CELEBRATE THEIR 150TH ANNIVERSARY IN 2025, WE LOOK BACK AT SOME OF THE MOST SIGNIFICANT MOMENTS IN THE CLUB'S HISTORY.

## FORMATION

It was in September 1875 that the Birmingham City Football Club story began. Much like several other professional football clubs in England, including Sheffield Wednesday, Tottenham Hotspur and rivals Aston Villa, Blues were established by members of a local cricket team. In Blues' case, it was cricketers from the Holy Trinity Church in Bordesley who decided to set up a football team as they wanted something to do during the winter months.

Under the name of 'Small Health Alliance', the team initially played on a piece of waste ground off Arthur Street, just a stone's throw away from St. Andrew's @ Knighthead Park. They moved to an enclosed field in Sparkbrook soon after and then to Muntz Street in 1877, which was the Club's home for the next 29 years prior to the construction and opening of St. Andrew's in 1906.

Blues joined the newly formed Football League Second Division in 1892 and were the division's inaugural champions. After two seasons in the First Division between 1893 and 1895 and further top-flight campaigns in 1901/02 and 1907/08, the Club achieved promotion again in 1921 and remained in the First Division for 18 consecutive seasons through until 1939.

During their early history, Blues changed their name to 'Small Heath' in 1888 and 'Birmingham' in 1905 before assuming the Club's current name in 1943.

## FA CUP FINALISTS

Victories over Liverpool, Port Vale, Watford, Chelsea, and Sunderland saw Birmingham reach their first FA Cup Final in 1931. Ernie Curtis and the Club's all-time leading goalscorer Joe Bradford were in great form en route to that final. Curtis netted six times – including a brace in the 2-0 semi-final win over Sunderland at Elland Road, Leeds – while Bradford scored seven times. Bradford also scored in the final against West Bromwich Albion on 25 April 1931 in front of a huge crowd of 92,406. Unfortunately, the Baggies ran out 2-1 winners.

Then-Blues manager Arthur Turner called on his side to produce a "90-minute performance" when they travelled to Torquay United in an FA Cup third round tie in January 1956 and his players duly obliged. A hat-trick from Eddy Brown, a brace from Peter Murphy and further strikes from Gordon Astall and Noel Kinsey sealed a 7-1 victory and started Birmingham's run to another FA Cup Final. Leyton Orient, West Bromwich Albion, Arsenal, and Sunderland proved no match for Turner's men, who took their place in the final against Manchester City at Wembley on 5 May 1956.

Alas, Blues once again fell to defeat in the showpiece occasion. The Cityzens' goalkeeper Bert Trautmann was the hero of the day, playing on for 17 minutes with a broken neck as his side won 3-1!

# EUROPEAN TRAILBLAZERS

Just 10 days after their defeat to Manchester City in the 1956 FA Cup Final, Birmingham City became the first-ever English club side to take part in a European competition – the Inter-Cities Fairs Cup, which is considered as the predecessor to the UEFA Cup (now known as the UEFA Europa League).

Blues drew 0-0 away to Inter Milan on their European debut and progressed to the semi-final of the 1955-58 competition before eventually losing 2-1 to Barcelona in a replay, after the original tie finished 4-4 on aggregate. Barca also proved to be Birmingham's nemesis in the competition in 1958-60, as they triumphed 4-1 on aggregate against Pat Beasley's Blues in the final.

Blues reached a second consecutive final in 1960-61 but were defeated by Roma while their fourth run in the competition was ended by Espanyol in the second round in 1961-62.

The Club's most recent campaign in European competition came in 2011/12, on the back of winning the 2011 Football League Cup (more on that shortly!). A 3-0 aggregate victory over C.D Nacional saw Blues qualify for the group stage of the UEFA Europa League. Amassing 10 points in six matches in Group H, Chris Hughton's side were so unlucky not to make it through to the knockout phase of the competition. Club Brugge and Braga progressed, finishing in the top two spots in the group with just a single point more than Blues.

# FOOTBALL LEAGUE CUP WINNERS

Birmingham City's first major trophy triumph came in 1962/63 as Gil Merrick's team won the Football League Cup – a competition that had been established just two seasons previously.

Blues scored no less than 24 goals en route to a two-legged final against rivals Aston Villa. This included a 5-0 win over Doncaster Rovers in the second round, a 5-1 victory over Barrow in a third-round replay and a 6-0 quarter-final thrashing of Manchester City. Blues beat Villa 3-1 in the first leg of the final, staged at St. Andrew's on 23 May 1963. Ken Leek scored twice while Jimmy Bloomfield was also on target. A goalless draw at Villa Park four days later sealed Blues' success.

Blues won the competition for a second time in 2010/11. Once again, the Club beat rivals Aston Villa on the way to glory, with a 2-1 fifth round triumph on 1 December 2010. Alex McLeish's side also saw off Rochdale, MK Dons, Brentford and West Ham United to take their place in a Wembley Stadium final against Arsenal on 27 February 2011. In front of a crowd of 88,851, Blues led after 28 minutes through a Nikola Žigić header. The Gunners levelled soon after through Robin van Persie but in the last minute of the 90, Obafemi Martins tapped the ball into an empty net after a mix-up between the Gunners' Wojciech Szczęsny and Laurent Koscielny, to the delight of the 30,000-plus Bluenoses inside the national stadium.

# THE £1M MAN

Trevor Francis sadly passed away on 24 July 2023 at the age of 69. Many Bluenoses fortunate enough to have seen him play would argue the Plymouth-born forward was the best player ever to ply his trade for Birmingham City.

Signing for Blues as a schoolboy in 1969, Francis scored 15 times in 16 matches for Blues before he had even celebrated his 17th birthday. This included a four-goal haul against Bolton Wanderers in a 4-0 Second Division victory at St. Andrew's on 20 February 1971. He starred in Freddie Goodwin's promotion-winning team in 1971/72, netting 12 times in 39 league matches. And in his first top-flight season in 1972/73, he scored six times in 31 matches. In 1977/78, Francis recorded his best seasonal tally of 29 goals and the following February transferred to Nottingham Forest to become Britain's first £1 million footballer.

A successful managerial career began at Queens Park Rangers and Sheffield Wednesday before an emotional return to St. Andrew's in 1996. During his five-year tenure, he guided Blues to the 2001 Football League Cup Final as well as three appearances in the First Division Play-Offs. Alas, he was unable to take Blues into the Premier League but certainly laid the foundations for the promotion which followed under Steve Bruce a season later.

Across 725 professional appearances, Francis scored 225 goals, with an astounding 113 of these coming in 330 treasured matches for Birmingham City.

Four months after heading to the City Ground, Trevor scored the winning goal in Forest's European Cup final triumph over Malmo while he won the European Super Cup and was a Football League Cup runner-up with Brian Clough's team the following season. He also played for Detroit Express, Manchester City, Sampdoria, Atalanta, Rangers, Queens Park Rangers, Wollongong Wolves and Sheffield Wednesday during his playing career and netted 12 times in 52 England appearances between 1977 and 1986.

# WE ARE PREMIER LEAGUE

A fourth consecutive First Division Play-Off campaign finally ended in success for Blues in 2001/02. After a fifth-place finish during the regular season, Steve Bruce's side saw off Millwall in the Play-Off semi-final to reach the final against Norwich City at the Millennium Stadium in Cardiff on 12 May 2002. After a goalless 90 minutes, Iwan Roberts scored for the Canaries in the first minute of extra-time but Geoff Horsfield levelled 11 minutes later. In the resulting penalty shootout, Stern John, Paul Devlin, Stan Lazaridis and Darren Carter all scored from the spot as Bruce's team won 4-2 on penalties to gain promotion to the Premier League for the first time.

And so began a four-season stay in the division. In Blues' first top-flight campaign since 1985/86, when they competed in the old First Division, Bruce's side finished in 13th position. Highlights of the season included a 3-0 victory over Aston Villa at St. Andrew's and a 2-0 win at Villa Park later in the campaign. Blues achieved comfortable, mid-table finishes in the following two seasons in the division - coming 10th and 12th - before suffering relegation in 2006. They bounced straight back to the top-flight by virtue of a second-place finish in the Championship in 2007 and did so once again in 2009, having been relegated the previous year.

Blues were again relegated in 2011 but at least had the consolation of the aforementioned Football League Cup triumph during the season.

# FA WOMEN'S SUPER LEAGUE FOUNDERS

Birmingham City Women were founded back in 1968 and enjoyed great early success, winning the Heart of England League/West Midland Regional League title five times during the 1970s and 1980s as well as reaching the semi-final of the Women's FA Cup in both 1974 and 1988.

In 1998, Birmingham City joined the newly created Midland Combination League. They won the division at their first attempt in 1998/99, gaining promotion to the FA Women's Premier League Northern Division. They were champions two seasons later and moved into the top-flight of women's league football, the FA Women's Premier League National Division, in 2002. The 2001/02 season also saw Blues upset top-flight Doncaster Belles 4-3 in the FA Women's Premier League Cup semi-final before going down to a 7-1 defeat to Fulham Ladies – the first professional women's club in Europe – in the final.

In 2011, Blues were one of eight founder members of the FA Women's Super League (FA WSL). They led the division for much of the campaign and reached the final of the Continental Cup but finished as runners-up to Arsenal in both competitions. They were also runners-up in both in 2012 in what was a memorable season, as the Blues embarked on a run to the Women's FA Cup Final, seeing off Liverpool, Sunderland and Bristol Academy along the way. A late Rachel Williams goal in the final against Chelsea at Ashton Gate, Bristol on 26 May 2012 forced extra-time. Chelsea reestablished their lead in the added period of 30 minutes, only for Player of the Match Karen Carney to level once again. Rachel Unitt, Jodie Taylor, and Carney all scored from the spot in the resulting penalty shootout as David Parker's side won Blues Women's first major trophy. Blues returned to the final in 2017 but lost on that occasion to Manchester City in front of a crowd of 35,271 at Wembley Stadium.

At the end of their 11th consecutive season in the FA WSL in 2021/22, Birmingham were relegated. They came agonisingly close to an instant return to the top-flight, finishing just one point off champions Bristol City in the 2022/23 FA Women's Championship with only one promotion spot up for grabs. Blues will be eyeing promotion to the top-flight again in 2024/25.

# HEY JUDE!

One of football's current global megastars, Jude Bellingham joined Birmingham City as an under-8 player and became Blues' youngest-ever first teamer when he made his senior debut against Portsmouth in the Football League Cup on 6 August 2019 aged 16 years and 38 days. The previous record was set by Blues legend Trevor Francis in 1970, at 16 years and 139 days.

Jude soon became Blues' youngest goalscorer too, netting the winner against Stoke City in the Championship on his home debut on 31 August 2019. The EFL's Young Player of the Month for November 2019, Bellingham's reputation swiftly grew during the 2019/20 season – so much so that Manchester United reportedly offered £20m for the player in January 2020.

Helping Blues avoid relegation on the final day of the COVID-19-disrupted 2019/20 season, Bellingham ended the campaign having scored four goals in 44 appearances in all competitions. At the EFL Awards at the end of the season, he was named both Championship Apprentice of the Year and EFL Young Player of the Season. Shortly before he departed for Borussia Dortmund for a reported £25m in July 2020, Blues retired the midfielder's number 22 squad number "to remember one of our own and to inspire others."

Bellingham won the DFB Pokal in his first season with Dortmund and moved to Real Madrid in 2023 for an incredible initial transfer fee of £103m, with the potential to rise to £133.9m due to add-ons. Blues received a sell-on fee as part of the transfer. In his debut season with Los Blancos, he scored 23 goals in 42 matches in all competitions as Real won La Liga, the Supercopa de España and the UEFA Champions League for a record 15th time. After starting in Real's 2-0 win over former club Dortmund in the final at Wembley Stadium on 1 June 2024, he headed to Germany where he was a key player in England's UEFA Euro 2024 campaign. Amongst his tournament highlights was a last-minute overhead kick in the Three Lions' 2-1 extra-time victory over Slovakia in the round of 16.

# A BRIGHT FUTURE

The future of Birmingham City Football Club was secured in July 2023 when US-based Shelby Companies Limited (SCL) completed its takeover of the Club. In an open letter to Blues fans, external Knighthead co-founder and co-chief executive Tom Wagner said; "The transition and implementation plans will take time.

"There will be bumps in the road, but I ask that you get behind the leadership team guiding the Club forward, be part of the alliance and continue to give every team that wears the shirt your passionate support."

A month later, NFL legend Tom Brady entered a partnership with Knighthead Capital Management LLC to become a minority owner of Birmingham City Ltd and became Chairman of the Club's new Advisory Board in the process.

Exciting developments on and off the pitch since SCL's takeover include the upgrading of facilities at St. Andrew's @ Knighthead Park (see pages 44-45), the purchase of land for a new stadium (see pages 46-47) and a host of new signings.

The future of Birmingham City Football Club is a bright one. So, here's to the next 150 years!

WILLUM WILLUMSSON

# BIRMINGHAM CITY FIXTURES

## 2024/25 SEASON

## JANUARY 2025

| Wed 1 | Jan: | Stockport County |
|-------|------|------------------|
| Sat 4 | Jan: | Wigan Athletic |
| **Sat 11** | **Jan:** | **Leyton Orient** |
| **Sat 18** | **Jan:** | **Exeter City** |
| Sat 25 | Jan: | Wrexham |
| Tue 28 | Jan: | Huddersfield Town |

## FEBRUARY 2025

| Sat 1 | Feb: | Rotherham United |
|-------|------|------------------|
| Sat 8 | Feb: | Peterborough United |
| **Sat 15** | **Feb:** | **Charlton Athletic** |
| Sat 22 | Feb: | Reading |

## MARCH 2025

| **Sat 1** | **Mar:** | **Wycombe Wanderers** |
|-----------|----------|-----------------------|
| Tue 4 | Mar: | Bolton Wanderers |
| **Sat 8** | **Mar:** | **Lincoln City** |
| Sat 15 | Mar: | Northampton Town |
| Sat 22 | Mar: | Stevenage |
| **Sat 29** | **Mar:** | **Shrewsbury Town** |

## APRIL 2025

| Tue 1 | Apr: | Bristol Rovers |
|-------|------|----------------|
| **Sat 5** | **Apr:** | **Barnsley** |
| Sat 12 | Apr: | Blackpool |
| **Fri 18** | **Apr:** | **Crawley Town** |
| Mon 21 | Apr: | Burton Albion |
| **Sat 26** | **Apr:** | **Mansfield Town** |

## MAY 2025

| Sat 3 | May: | Cambridge United |
|-------|------|------------------|

Matches in 2025 only. **Bold** denotes a home fixture. All fixtures are subject to change.
Up to date fixture information can be found at BCFC.com

# MEN'S PLAYER PROFILES

### NEW SIGNING
# RYAN ALLSOP

A boyhood Birmingham City fan, Ryan signed for Blues in June 2024 from Hull City. The experienced goalkeeper has made over 350 appearances during his career so far at the time of writing, including 38 games between the sticks for the Tigers in 2023/24. His other previous clubs include Leyton Orient, AFC Bournemouth, Coventry City (loan), Blackpool (loan), Wycombe Wanderers, Derby County and Cardiff City.

### NEW SIGNING
# BAILEY PEACOCK-FARRELL

Goalkeeper Bailey joined Blues on a four-year deal from Burnley in July 2024. He spent 2023/24 on loan at Aarhus GF where his 11 clean sheets helped them to a fifth-place finish in the Danish Superliga. Bailey – who has 46 Northern Ireland Caps at the time of writing – began his career with Leeds United. He went on loan to York City before completing his move to the Clarets in 2019 with whom he won the Championship title in 2022/23.

# BRAD MAYO

Twelve months after signing his first professional contract with Blues, Brad agreed a further two-year deal with the Club in June 2024. A product of their Academy, the goalkeeper had an impressive 2023/24 season with the Under-21s, starting 34 of their 40 matches in all competitions and recording nine clean sheets as Steve Spooner's side reached the Professional Development League National Final. He was also named in five matchday squads for the Men's first team.

## ETHAN LAIRD

Ethan featured in 25 games for Blues in his debut season with the Club after signing from Manchester United in July 2023. He rose through the ranks at Old Trafford after joining the Red Devils at the age of 10 and went on to make his first team debut in the UEFA Europa League against Astana in November 2019. Loans with Milton Keynes Dons, Swansea City, AFC Bournemouth, and Queens Park Rangers followed, before his move to St. Andrew's @ Knighthead Park.

## LEE BUCHANAN

Lee began his career with Derby County for whom he made 75 first team appearances between 2019 and 2022 before moving to Bundesliga side Werder Bremen. During his single season in Germany, he featured in 23 matches in all competitions and was named 'Bundesliga Rookie Player of the Month' in August 2022 after scoring in a memorable 3-2 win at Borussia Dortmund. The defender returned to England in the summer of 2023 to sign for Blues and he made 35 appearances in all competitions in his debut season.

## DION SANDERSON

A key player at the heart of Blues' defence and their Captain for 2023/24, Wednesfield-born Dion made a permanent move to B9 in July 2023 after enjoying two loan spells at the Club from Wolverhampton Wanderers - whose academy he joined as an eight-year-old. He made 16 appearances for Blues in the first half of the 2021/22 season and then scored twice in 34 appearances during a second loan at St. Andrew's @ Knighthead Park in 2022/23. The defender has also featured for Cardiff City, Sunderland, and Queens Park Rangers in his career so far.

## JOSH WILLIAMS

Josh joined Blues when he was just eight years old, and after working his way through the ranks he made his senior debut against Plymouth Argyle in the FA Cup in January 2022. The versatile defender went on to feature a further seven times for Birmingham during 2022/23 and signed a new contract with the Club at the end of that campaign. In September 2023, Josh joined League One club Cheltenham Town on loan until January 2024, making nine appearances for the Robins.

NEW SIGNING
# ALEX COCHRANE

Alex began his career with his hometown club Brighton & Hove Albion, where he progressed through the ranks to make his first-team debut in the League Cup against Aston Villa in September 2019. He had loan spells with East Grinstead Town and Belgian side Union SG before spending the 2021/22 season with Heart of Midlothian – a move which became permanent at the end of that campaign. The defender made a total of 96 appearances for Hearts prior to his move to Blues in July 2024.

NEW SIGNING
# CHRISTOPH KLARER

Defender Christoph joined Blues from Darmstadt 98 in July 2024, putting pen-to-paper on a three-year contract. During his single season at Darmstadt in 2023/24, the former Southampton and Fortuna Düsseldorf player missed just four top-flight league matches. Capped 12 times by Austria at under-21 level, the Böheimkirchen-born centre-back has also appeared for his country at all levels between under-15 and under-19.

NEW LOAN SIGNING
# TAYLOR GARDNER-HICKMAN

Taylor joined West Bromwich Albion's academy when he was just seven years of age. He progressed through the Baggies' youth ranks to eventually play 60 senior competitive matches between 2021 and 2024. Loaned to Bristol City during the 2023/24 season, the Telford-born midfielder made his move to Ashton Gate permanent in January 2024 while he signed on a season-long loan with Blues in August 2024.

NEW LOAN SIGNING
# BEN DAVIES

Ben arrived at St. Andrew's @ Knighthead Park in August 2024 for the seventh loan of his career having previously represented York City, Tranmere Rovers, Southport, Newport County, Fleetwood Town and Sheffield United on a temporary basis. In between times, he has been under contract at Preston North End and Liverpool, while he has been a Rangers player since 2022. The experienced Cumbrian defender can operate either at centre-back or left-back.

NEW LOAN SIGNING
# ALFONS SAMPSTED

Alfons joined Blues on a season-long loan from Dutch side FC Twente in August 2024 and made his debut for the Club against Charlton Athletic in the Carabao Cup that same month. The Iceland international has won over 20 caps for his country to date and has also plied his trade for clubs in Iceland, Sweden and Norway.

# ★★★★★ MIDFIELDERS ★★★★★

# KRYSTIAN BIELIK

Krystian signed permanently for Blues in the summer of 2023, following two loan spells with the Club - in 2017 and for the 2022/23 season. His 39 appearances in 2023/24, either at centre-back or as a defensive midfielder, brought his total tally in blue to 86. The Poland international, who has also played for the likes of Legia Warsaw, Charlton Athletic (loan) and Derby County during his career, has 11 caps at the time of writing since making his debut against Slovenia in a Euro 2020 qualifier in September 2019.

# PAIK SEUNG-HO

A South Korea international, Paik joined Birmingham City in January 2024 following three years at Jeonbuk Hyundai Motors in his homeland where he won the K. League and domestic cup. He played in 18 matches in all competitions for Blues in his first half-season with the Club, scoring once. Paik featured for his country at the 2022 FIFA World Cup, and in March 2024 received his first senior call-up for a year, for 2026 World Cup qualifiers against Thailand, winning his 16th and 17th caps in the process.

# ALFIE CHANG

Following a breakthrough season in 2022/23, where he featured in 17 matches in all competitions for Blues, Alfie found himself sidelined for seven months following a serious knee injury sustained in training in August 2023. During his recovery, the midfielder – who made progress through the ranks to make his first team debut against Fulham in 2021 – signed a contract extension with the Club which will keep him at St. Andrew's @ Knighthead Park until 2026.

# BRANDON KHELA

A regular in Blues' matchday squad for the first few months of the 2023/24 campaign, Brandon made his Championship debut from the substitutes' bench in a 4-1 home win over Huddersfield Town in October 2023. Just two months earlier, he'd become the first British South Asian to feature in a competitive match for Birmingham City in a 2-0 Carabao Cup win at Cheltenham Town. After those two first team appearances, the midfielder went on loan to Scottish Premiership club Ross County in January 2024, until the end of that campaign, where he played 15 times and netted once.

# JOSH HOME

A strong leader in the centre of midfield, Josh captained the Under-21s to the Professional Development League National Final in May 2024, less than a year after signing his first professional contract with the Club ahead of the 2023/24 season. Prior to his move to B9 in 2021, Josh was on the books of his hometown team Newcastle United.

NEW SIGNING

# MARC LEONARD

Glasgow-born Marc signed for Blues in July 2024 from Brighton & Hove Albion. A product of Rangers' youth system, he then spent four years with Heart of Midlothian before joining the Seagulls' Academy in 2018, making his professional debut in the League Cup against Cardiff City in August 2021. The midfielder spent back-to-back seasons on loan at Northampton Town where he helped the club secure promotion to Sky Bet League One in 2022/23 and missed just one league match in 2023/24. Marc had been capped on seven occasions for Scotland Under-21s at the time of writing.

NEW SIGNING

# WILLUM WILLUMSSON

Iceland international Willum was Blues' fifth signing of the summer 2024 transfer window, joining from Dutch outfit Go Ahead Eagles. In 2023/24 he played a vital part in his club's top-10 finish in the Eredivisie, defying all expectations to qualify for the UEFA Conference League. Willum has also turned out for BATE Borisov in Belarus and Breiðablik during his career, and at the time of writing has nine international caps to his name.

NEW SIGNING
# SCOTT WRIGHT

After more than three seasons with Rangers, winger Scott Wright signed for Blues on 2024 summer transfer deadline day. During his time at Ibrox, Wright helped deliver a 55th Scottish Premiership title in 2020/21 while he scored in their 2-0 victory over Heart of Midlothian in the 2022 Scottish Cup Final. The former Aberdeen man also won the Scottish League Cup with Rangers during the 2023/24 season.

NEW SIGNING
# TOMOKI IWATA

On summer transfer deadline day 2024, Blues completed the signing of Tomoki Iwata from Celtic on a three-year contract. Tomoki spent the previous 21 months playing his football at Parkhead, initially joining on loan during the managerial reign of Ange Postecoglou. Across 42 appearances for the Hoops, the four-time Japanese international won two Scottish Premiership titles, two Scottish Cups and one Scottish League Cup.

# ★ ★ ★ ★ ★ FORWARDS ★ ★ ★ ★ ★ ★

NEW LOAN SIGNING
# LUKE HARRIS

Luke joined Blues on a season-long-loan from Premier League side Fulham ahead of the start of the 2024/25 campaign. Previously loaned to Exeter City during the second half of the 2023/24 season, the attacking midfielder has played for Wales between under-17 and under-21 level while he was called up to the senior team for UEFA Nations League matches against Belgium and Poland back in September 2022.

# LUKAS JUTKIEWICZ

2024/25 is Lukas' ninth season with Blues after the Club Captain signed a one-year deal in July 2024. The striker has made 331 appearances and scored 67 goals for the Club as of the end of 2023/24, after initially joining on loan from Burnley in the summer of 2016. He was named Blues' Player of the Year in 2020 and has been their top goalscorer in three campaigns.

# KESHI ANDERSON

Keshi featured in 24 games for Blues in 2023/24 with his performances earning him a contract extension at the end of the campaign. The striker had initially joined on a one-year deal in July 2023 after his contract at Blackpool came to an end. Keshi began his career at non-league side Barton Rovers where his prolific goalscoring form caught the eye of Crystal Palace and he signed for the Eagles in 2015. Loan spells at Doncaster Rovers, Bolton Wanderers, Northampton Town, and Swindon Town followed with the latter signing him permanently in January 2018, before his move to the Tangerines.

NEW SIGNING

# ALFIE MAY

Twenty-seven goals in all competitions for Charlton Athletic in 2023/24 saw Alfie claim the Sky Bet League One Golden Boot and win the Addicks' Player of the Season. The striker signed for Blues on the back of that impressive campaign, in July 2024. Prior to his single season with Charlton, he played 165 games for Cheltenham Town with whom he won the League Two title in 2020/21, and he's also represented Doncaster Rovers as well as several non-league teams between 2012 and 2017.

NEW SIGNING

# EMIL HANSSON

Emil was a key performer for Heracles in 2023/24 as his 16 goals and 19 assists in 36 Eerste Divisie appearances helped his side to the league title and promotion back to the top flight of Dutch football. In July 2024, Blues announced they had agreed to sign the former Brann, Feyenoord, RKC Waalwijk (loan), Hannover 96 and Fortuna Sittard player on a three-year contract. The Bergen-born winger has represented both Sweden and his native Norway at youth level.

NEW SIGNING

# LYNDON DYKES

Born in Gold Coast, Australia to Scottish parents, Lyndon previously played for Australian clubs Mudgeeraba, Merrimac, Redlands United and Surfers Paradise Apollo while he had spells in Scotland with Queen of the South and Livingston. The 6ft 2in forward moved to Queens Park Rangers in August 2020 and went on to score 37 goals in 166 appearances prior to joining Blues on a three-year contract in August 2024.

## NEW SIGNING
# JAY STANSFIELD

Jay signed for Blues from Fulham on summer transfer deadline day 2024 for a record fee for an EFL League One club. The forward enjoyed a memorable loan spell at St. Andrew's @ Knighthead Park during the 2023/24 season, when he scored 13 goals in 47 matches in all competitions. He picked up all five Men's awards at the BCFC Awards 2024, namely; Supporters' Player of the Season, Players' Player of the Season, Young Player of the Season, Top Goalscorer and Goal of the Season. On his return to the Second City, Jay was handed Blues' number 28 shirt.

## NEW SIGNING
# AYUMU YOKOYAMA

Ayumu joined Blues from Sagan Tosu in August 2024. He departed Sagan having featured in 24 of the club's opening 25 matches of the J1 League season, during which time he had scored five goals and made three assists. The Japan youth international made his Blues debut in the 3-2 away win at Wycombe Wanderers on 17 August 2024.

# WOMEN'S PLAYER PROFILES

## ★★★★★ GOALIES ★★★★★

### LUCY THOMAS

A fantastic season between the sticks for Blues in 2023/24 saw Lucy being called up to the England senior squad for the first time, for UEFA Euro 2025 qualifying games in the summer of 2024. She played every minute of Birmingham's 22 Barclays Women's Championship fixtures, keeping nine clean sheets, and featured in all three of their Adobe Women's FA Cup games and one FA Women's Continental League Cup match. The shot-stopper, who signed for Blues from Coventry United in July 2022, also previously played for London City Lionesses and Oxford United.

### CHARLOTTE CLARKE

Charlotte joined Blues ahead of the 2023/24 season, on the back of having won the Supporters' Player of the Season award at West Bromwich Albion. In her debut season at St. Andrew's @ Knighthead Park, the young goalkeeper made two appearances in the Conti Cup – against Brighton & Hove Albion and Charlton Athletic – making some fine saves in both games.

## ★★★★★ DEFENDERS ★★★★★

### NEVE HERRON

After signing for Blues from Sunderland in the summer of 2023, centre-back Neve made 26 appearances in all competitions in her debut season in B9 and was a key member in the heart of Birmingham's defence. She registered two assists during a standout performance in a 4-0 defeat of Reading in March 2024 and received her first call-up to the England Under-23s squad during the campaign. Neve was voted Young Player of the Season and Players' Player of the Season at Awards24.

# LOUISE QUINN

On the back of playing in all three of the Republic of Ireland's 2023 FIFA Women's World Cup games, Louise continued to be an important player for her Club throughout 2023/24. Louise made 21 appearances in all competitions, which included 16 starts, and netted once – against Crystal Palace at St. Andrew's @ Knighthead Park in September 2023. Prior to joining Birmingham in 2021, Louise plied her trade in Italy with Fiorentina, and she has also played for clubs including Arsenal, Swedish side Eskilstuna United and Peamount United in her native homeland. At the time of writing, she has 119 international caps and 16 goals.

# GEMMA LAWLEY

Gemma netted twice in 24 appearances in all competitions for Blues in 2023/24, forming a strong partnership with Neve Herron and Louise Quinn in Birmingham's defence. Her performances in November 2023 saw her named Barclays Women's Championship Player of the Month. Born in Birmingham on 15 September 2002, Gemma joined Blues' Academy at the age of 16 and by the end of the 2023/24 campaign she had made more than 75 appearances for the Club.

# MARTHA HARRIS

Injury restricted Martha's appearances to 15 in all competitions in 2023/24, but the right-back still scored two superb strikes, the first in a 4-0 win against Sheffield United which won her the Goal of the Season accolade at Awards24. Her second effort was another memorable volley into the top corner as Blues beat Women's Super League side West Ham 2-1 in the Conti Cup group stage. The first-ever winner of the PFA Women's Young Player of the Year in 2013/14 whilst she was playing for Liverpool, Martha has previously represented England between under-19 and under-23 level.

# ELLIE MASON

Ellie had an impressive debut season in B9 with one goal and one assist in 20 appearances altogether for Blues after joining the Club from Lewes – where she won the Barclays Women's Championship Goal of the Season Award in 2022/23. The defender started her career at Watford, and after a four-year spell at Chelsea, returned to the Hornets in 2015. The versatile player has also had stints at Millwall Lionesses, Yeovil Town and London City Lionesses during her career. Originally capped by Gibraltar, Ellie changed her international allegiance to Northern Ireland in 2022, for whom she has played twice at the time of writing.

# REBECCA HOLLOWAY

Having spent 18 months out in the United States with Racing Louisville, Rebecca returned to St. Andrew's @ Knighthead Park in January 2024, for her second spell with Blues. After making a total of 65 appearances during her first stint in B9, between 2019 and 2022, the defender went on to make a further seven appearances, picking up one assist, in the second half of the 2023/24 campaign. Rebecca has 24 caps and three goals for Northern Ireland at the time of writing and featured in all three of their Group A matches at the UEFA European Championships in 2022, their first major tournament.

# SIOBHAN WILSON

After nine months out with an Anterior Cruciate Ligament injury that she suffered in April 2023, Siobhan put pen-to-paper on a new one-year contract in February 2024, keeping her at Blues until the end of the 2024/25 campaign. The defender went on to make three appearances from the substitutes' bench towards the end of 2023/24, to add to the 24 she made in her debut season before getting injured. Siobhan joined Birmingham in July 2022, off the back of a standout campaign with Crystal Palace, where she finished as their joint-top goalscorer with five goals in 2021/22.

# REBECCA MCKENNA ★ NEW SIGNING ★

Blues signed Rebecca on a two-year deal in July 2024 after the defender departed fellow Championship side Charlton Athletic. She featured 25 times for the Addicks in all competitions in 2023/24 helping them secure a second-place finish. Prior to that, the Northern Ireland international spent two seasons with Lewes whom she joined from Belfast-based outfit Linfield in 2021. Rebecca represented her country at Euro 2022, Northern Ireland's first-ever major tournament, and has also been a mainstay in their defence for Women's World Cup and Euro qualifying campaigns.

# ★★★★★ MIDFIELDERS ★★★★★

# CHRISTIE HARRISON-MURRAY

Blues' Team Captain for the 2023/24 season, Christie played in all but one of their Championship games and netted once in a 1-1 draw with Sunderland in October 2023. The experienced midfielder, who joined Birmingham on a free transfer from Liverpool in the summer of 2020, has played more than 90 games in royal blue at the time of writing. Since making her international debut for Scotland in 2010, Christie, a typical 'number 10', who likes to operate in advance midfield or deep-lying forward positions, has been capped 80 times by her country and represented them at the FIFA Women's World Cup in 2019.

# LILY AGG

After an impressive debut season with Blues in 2023/24, Lily signed a new contract with the Club in May 2024. The midfielder scored six goals in 25 appearances in all competitions, including against WSL side West Ham United as Blues triumphed 2-1 in their final Conti Cup group game. At Awards 24, Lily picked up two prizes, Supporters' Player of the Season and Top Goalscorer - the latter jointly with Libby Smith. The Brighton-born player has 17 caps and three goals for the Republic of Ireland national team up to and including their 1-0 defeat to Sweden a Women's Euro 2025 qualifier in June 2024. She also played for her country at the 2023 FIFA Women's World Cup.

## CHO SO-HYUN

Cho put pen-to-paper on a new contract with Blues in March 2024, which will see her remain at the Club until at least June 2025. The midfielder - who has also played for West Ham United and Tottenham Hotspur in the WSL - made 13 appearances in blue during 2023/24 and netted the winning goal against London City Lionesses in the Women's Championship in January 2024. In February 2024, Cho picked up her 150th international cap for South Korea in a friendly against Portugal. In doing so, she became only the second player to reach that amount for her country.

## JAMIE FINN

Dublin-born Jamie has been capped 15 times by the Republic of Ireland at the time of writing, with the majority of those coming while a Blues player. She joined the West Midlands club from Shelbourne in the summer of 2021, making 56 appearances in total during her first two seasons in B9. Jamie - who predominantly plays at right-back - followed that up with a further 20 appearances in 2023/24 before suffering an ACL injury while on international duty in February 2024.

## LUCY QUINN

Lucy reached a special milestone at Blues during 2023/24 – her 100th appearance for the Club! It came in their game against Charlton Athletic in September 2023 in what is her second spell in B9. Having initially joined the Club back in 2017 from Yeovil Town, the striker spent two years with Blues before moving to Tottenham Hotspur. Two seasons later she moved back to the Second City and has become a key player upfront for Birmingham – featuring in every one of their league and cup games in 2023/24 and netting twice. In October 2023, Lucy was named Barclays Women's Championship Player of the Month. She's also a regular for the Republic of Ireland Women's team and played in all four of their UEFA Women's Euro 2025 qualifiers up to and including their 1-0 defeat to Sweden in June 2024 to bring her caps tally to 24.

## CHARLIE DEVLIN

Charlie joined Blues on a permanent deal in July 2023 having spent the 2022/23 season on loan from Leicester City. The midfielder featured 22 times for Birmingham in all competitions in 2023/24 and scored four goals, including a brace in their 2-1 win over Reading in November 2023. Devlin's career started at the Millwall Centre of Excellence, before making the switch to Arsenal, where she signed her first professional contract. She has also turned out for Millwall Lionesses, Manchester United and Charlton Athletic during her career.

## ASHANTI AKPAN ⭐ NEW LOAN SIGNING ⭐

Ashanti joined Blues Women on a season-long loan from Barclays Women's Super League champions Chelsea in August 2024. The midfielder has been with the Londoners since the age of seven and signed her first professional contract with them in December 2023, nine months after making her first team debut from the bench in a Women's FA Cup tie against Reading. Ashanti has represented England at youth level and was in the squad for the 2024 UEFA Women's Under-19 European Championships as the side made it to the semi-finals.

# FORWARDS ★★★★★

## LIBBY SMITH

Libby's six strikes in 23 appearances in all competitions in 2023/24 saw her finish the campaign as Blues' joint-top goalscorer, along with Lily Agg. The forward arrived at St. Andrew's @ Knighthead Park from Leicester City in 2021, whom she helped gain promotion to the FA WSL in 2021. The versatile player, who can also operate as a winger, has also represented England's youth sides from under-15s to under-19s level, including appearances as captain of the Young Lionesses.

## JADE PENNOCK

Jade followed up an outstanding 2022/23 season, netting 11 times in 22 league matches and winning the Barclays Women's Championship Player of the Season accolade, with a further 16 appearances in all competitions in 2023/24, as a hamstring injury limited the attacker's game-time. She scored once for Blues during the campaign – in a 3-1 defeat of Durham in November 2023. Jade joined Birmingham in 2021 from Sheffield United, and she has also featured for Doncaster Belles and played college football in the United States.

## LOUANNE WORSEY

A product of Blues' Academy, Louanne signed her first professional contract with the Club in the summer of 2023 after making four appearances during the 2021/22 season and a further three in 2022/23. In September 2023, the young forward - who is a lifelong Bluenose - joined Nottingham Forest of the Women's National League North on loan until the end of 2023/24 to gain more first team experience.

## IVANA FUSO

Ivana joined Blues for a Club-record fee in September 2023 and went on to make 17 appearances in all competitions and netted four times in her debut campaign. She spent the 2022/23 season on loan from Manchester United at Frauen Bundesliga side Bayer Leverkusen, where she made 12 appearances in total, scoring once. The forward started her career at SC Freiburg and played for FC Basel before moving to Manchester in 2020. Ivana spent her youth international career with Germany between under-15 and under-19 level before switching her allegiance to her country of birth, Brazil, for her senior international career, making her debut for the Seleção against Argentina in February 2021 in the SheBelieves Cup.

## CHOE YU-RI

Yu-ri netted her first goal for Blues in their 2-0 victory over MK Dons in the third round of the Women's FA Cup in December 2023, just three months after joining the Club from WK League side Hyundai Steel Red Angels, where she had been since 2021. The South Korean forward featured in 17 games for Birmingham altogether in 2023/24 after making her debut in a 2-1 league victory over Reading in November 2023. Since making her national team debut back in 2014, Yu-ri has gone on to score 11 times in 63 appearances for her country at the time of writing which included all three of South Korea's group stage matches at the Women's World Cup in 2023.

## AVA BAKER ✦ NEW SIGNING ✦

Ava became Blues Women's first signing of the 2024 summer transfer window. The Leicester-born winger came through the ranks at her hometown club before making her first team debut for the Foxes just three days after her 16th birthday in an FA Women's Continental League Cup match against Manchester City. She made 28 appearances in total for Leicester, scoring her first Women's Super League goal on the final day of the 2022/23 season against Brighton & Hove Albion which ultimately secured the Foxes' WSL survival. Ava has represented England at under-17 and under-19 levels.

## TEGAN MCGOWAN ✦ NEW SIGNING ✦

Just 24 hours after the arrival of Rebecca McKenna in July 2024, her former Charlton teammate Tegan also signed for Blues. In her two years with the Addicks, the forward scored five goals in 25 appearances in all competitions. As a youngster, Tegan spent six years at Chelsea's academy while also training with the first team before making the move to Charlton in 2022, where she signed her first professional contract. The versatile player has also represented Wales at under-19 level.

## SIMONE MAGILL ✦ NEW SIGNING ✦

Experienced international forward Simone signed for Blues on a two-year contract in August 2024 on the back of her departure from the Club's Second City rivals, Aston Villa, in the Barclays Women's Super League. Prior to her two seasons as a Villan, the Magherafelt-born player spent almost 10 years with Everton, for whom she made over 150 appearances in all competitions. At the point at which she put pen-to-paper on her Blues contract, the forward had scored 24 goals in 78 appearances for Northern Ireland.

2023/24 marked Birmingham City's 13th consecutive season in the Sky Bet Championship. It was an eventful campaign for Blues, who got off to a fantastic start, picking up 10 points from their first four league matches. They recorded notable wins over Leeds United and local rivals West Bromwich Albion during the campaign and reached the fourth round of the Emirates FA Cup. Jay Stansfield, on loan from Fulham, was Blues' top scorer with 13 goals in all competitions.

# AUGUST

Blues picked up a point at Swansea City on the opening day of the 2023/24 season. They had a few chances in the first half before new signing Siriki Dembélé – who'd joined from AFC Bournemouth – finally broke the deadlock just before half-time when he stroked the ball home from a Keshi Anderson pass. Swansea equalised through Jerry Yates and Birmingham came so close to a winner late on, but Swans goalkeeper Carl Rushworth pulled off a fine save to deny Ivan Šunjić.

They made a winning start in the Carabao Cup as Juninho Bacuna scored a brace against League One side Cheltenham Town in the first round on 8 August 2023. The midfielder put Blues ahead with a deflected shot on 24 minutes before his lovely right-foot effort found the top corner just eight minutes later to set up a second-round tie with Cardiff City.

Blues' first league win came against Leeds United four days later, and they certainly left it late to seal all three points. The referee pointed to the penalty spot in the ninetieth minute of the game after Daniel James fouled Ethan Laird, and Lukas Jutkiewicz – who'd only been substituted on two minutes previously – scored the resulting spot-kick to give Blues victory. After the game, boss John Eustace dedicated their win to Club legend Trevor Francis, who passed away in July 2023.

Birmingham extended their unbeaten run with a 2-0 victory at Bristol City to climb up to third in the Championship table. Substitute Kōji Miyoshi scored his first goal for the Club in first-half added time – a perfect volley high into the net from an Anderson corner – before Jutkiewicz doubled Blues' advantage from close range with six minutes of the 90 remaining.

Jay Stansfield netted in stoppage time on his Blues debut against Plymouth Argyle to make it three wins in three Championship games for Eustace's side. The forward, on loan from Fulham received a Goal of the Month nomination for his stunning volley in the 96th minute to get the victory, after Ryan Hardie's strike cancelled out Scott Hogan's early opener for Blues.

Hogan was on the scoresheet once again four days later, but his strike in the Carabao Cup second round tie with Cardiff City proved only a consolation as a 10-man Blues went down 3-1 to exit the competition.

# SEPTEMBER

A 53rd-minute strike from Stansfield earnt a point for Birmingham City against Millwall to extend their unbeaten start in the league to five matches.

Full-back Cody Drameh was handed his debut after arriving at the Club the previous day on loan from Leeds, in what proved an eventful game at St. Andrew's @ Knighthead Park. The Lions went in front through Kevin Nisbet's free-kick before Anderson was brought down inside the area in first-half injury time and Hogan stepped up to take the penalty – only for his effort to be saved by Matija Sarkic.

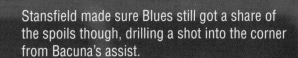

Stansfield made sure Blues still got a share of the spoils though, drilling a shot into the corner from Bacuna's assist.

Watford inflicted Blues' first league defeat of the season with two late goals in a competitive encounter at Vicarage Road. Hogan and Stansfield had the visitors' best chances, with Jay even hitting the post in the second half, but 10-man Blues couldn't find the target.

A narrow 2-1 defeat at Preston North End under the floodlights – where Stansfield scored his third goal in five appearances – was followed by a goalless draw with Queens Park Rangers. Both sides had plenty of chances but their defences – and goalkeepers – were in inspired form as Blues remained unbeaten in the league at St. Andrew's @ Knighthead Park. Blues' final fixture of September saw them lose 2-0 to Norwich City.

# OCTOBER

Back at home and back to winning ways, Birmingham scored seven goals in their next two games. Dembélé bagged a brace and Miyoshi and Jordan James were also on the scoresheet in a comfortable 4-1 victory over Huddersfield Town to move back up to 10th in the table. That improved to fifth, as Blues came from behind to beat West Brom 3-1 to record their fourth consecutive victory over the Baggies.

John Swift netted for the visitors after just six minutes but Blues were back level midway through the first half when Bacuna coolly converted a penalty following a foul on Miyoshi. A well-worked set piece led to Blues' second as Drameh set up Sanderson who headed home past Alex Palmer in the Baggies goal to give Blues a 2-1 lead at the break.

Gary Gardner – having been introduced from the bench – put the game to bed three minutes before added time with a superb free-kick over a well-assembled Baggies wall.

A change in management saw John Eustace replaced by Wayne Rooney during the international break. It wasn't an easy start to life in B9 for the former England striker as Blues were narrowly beaten 1-0 by Middlesbrough at the Riverside before losing 2-0 at home to Hull City.

They put in a spirited second-half performance against eventual promotion winners Southampton and when Stansfield came off the bench to pull it back to 2-1 just before the hour mark, it looked like game on. But Saints made sure of victory through Adam Armstrong.

# NOVEMBER

Rooney picked up his first point as Blues boss with a 2-2 draw against Ipswich Town, but his side would have been disappointed to let slip a two-goal lead. They made a bright start at St. Andrew's @ Knighthead Park with Stansfield scoring from close range in the first half and their advantage was doubled shortly after the break when Town's Cameron Burgess deflected the ball into his own net. But two late goals from the Tractor Boys denied Blues all three points.

Miyoshi scored Blues' only goal in a 3-1 defeat to Sunderland before they staged a hard-fought comeback to win 2-1 against Sheffield Wednesday. George Byers' 45th-minute opener was cancelled out by a stunning Bacuna volley and substitute Jordan James netted the winner after he rounded the Wednesday keeper in the 81st minute to tap the ball home.

Blackburn Rovers ran out 4-2 winners at Ewood Park at the end of November despite Dembélé scoring a brace for Blues.

# DECEMBER

A goalless draw against Rotherham United and 2-0 loss at Coventry City was followed by a 1-0 victory away at Cardiff City. Blues began the match brightly and came close through Stansfield, but his shot went just wide of the post. A quick counter-attack on the stroke of half-time saw them take the lead through Bacuna as he lofted the ball over Cardiff's goalkeeper before slotting it into an empty net, and Rooney's side showed resilience to see the game out.

Blues were unlucky not to pick up any points from their home tie with eventual Championship champions Leicester City. It finished 2-3 in B9 with James netting both of Birmingham's goals – one in either half – but they couldn't find the all-important third.

The travelling Bluenoses watched a six-goal thriller at Home Park shortly before Christmas. Having netted the winner late on against the Pilgrims back in August, Stansfield headed home for Blues' opener on 15 minutes before James made it two with a volley that bounced in off the bar. Plymouth equalised but Birmingham increased their lead through Bacuna. A Marc Roberts own-goal gave the hosts their second of the day before Morgan Whittaker scored late on to give Plymouth a share of the spoils.

Stansfield added another to his goal tally during Blues' Boxing Day clash with Stoke City but the Potters won 3-1 at St. Andrew's @ Knighthead Park and Blues ended the year with a 0-0 draw against Bristol City at home.

# JANUARY

It was a New Year's Day to forget for Blues as they were beaten 3-0 by Leeds, but things improved as the month went on. Rooney departed St. Andrew's @ Knighthead Park, and under interim boss Steve Spooner they drew 1-1 with Hull City in the third round of the FA Cup – Jutkiewicz scored on 18 minutes – before goals from Stansfield and Miyoshi gave

them a 2-1 victory in the replay on 16 January 2024 under new permanent manager Tony Mowbray. Three days previously, Dembélé and James had both been on target in a 2-2 draw with Swansea City at St. Andrew's @ Knighthead Park in the league.

Under Mowbray, they also got revenge over Stoke City for the previous month's defeat by triumphing 2-1 at the bet365 Stadium thanks to goals from Stansfield and Bacuna. Their FA Cup journey came to an end at the hands of fellow Championship side Leicester City in the fourth round (0-3).

# FEBRUARY

Back-to-back defeats against West Brom and Sheffield Wednesday were followed by consecutive victories for Blues. QPR loanee Andre Dozzell's strike on 77 minutes was enough to seal all three points against Blackburn, and Mowbray named an unchanged starting XI for their home game against Sunderland, which Blues won 2-1. James scored on the hour-mark after the Black Cats had taken the lead through Jack Clarke, and Miyoshi grabbed the winner 10 minutes from time.

James was Blues' scorer as they lost 3-1 to Ipswich to round off the month after Mowbray announced he was temporarily stepping away from on-site management to undergo medical treatment, with his number two, Mark Venus, taking charge instead.

# MARCH

March was an extremely difficult month for Blues. Mowbray took formal medical leave and Gary Rowett rejoined the Club as interim manager until the end of the campaign. On the pitch, the side picked up just one point from six games.

# APRIL

Games came thick and fast for Blues in April, kicking off with a vital 1-0 win over Preston as striker Stansfield found the net on 68 minutes.

The England Under-23s international was on target against Leicester five days later for his 12th goal of the season, but couldn't prevent his side going down to a 2-1 defeat at the King Power Stadium. They also lost 1-0 at home against Cardiff but bounced back immediately with their first league win over Coventry City in 13 years. Bobby Thomas' own goal gave Blues the lead inside 15 minutes and Ivan Šunjić's volley just before half-time doubled their advantage. Stansfield made it 3-0 from close range after being set up by Tyler Roberts.

Blues' final two games of April were both draws, 0-0 away at Rotherham and 1-1 against Huddersfield Town.

# MAY

Birmingham City concluded their season in front of 27,680 fans at St. Andrew's @ Knighthead Park with a 1-0 win over Norwich - Paik Seung-ho's 55th-minute goal was his first in English football. Sadly, the victory wasn't enough to lift Blues above 22nd position in the table, and their stay in the second tier came to an end.

**ALFIE MAY**

# WOMEN'S REVIEW
## OF THE SEASON 2023/24

Blues came fifth in the Barclays Women's Championship in 2023/24, picking up 11 wins and three draws, and made it to the fifth round of the Adobe Women's FA Cup.

★★★☆ **WOMEN'S CHAMPIONSHIP** ★★★☆

Darren Carter's side lost their first two games of the season - 1-0 at Blackburn Rovers on the opening day and then 2-1 to Crystal Palace as Louise Quinn's header in added time at St. Andrew's @ Knighthead Park proved only a consolation.

They picked up their first point of the campaign in a goalless draw with Lewes and were narrowly beaten 1-0 by Charlton Athletic before recording their first win (3-1) at Southampton. Libby Smith netted a brace and Saints' Rosie Parnell deflected Claudia Walker's cross into her own net for Blues' goals at Snows Stadium.

Next up was Sunderland, and Christie Harrison-Murray's 78th-minute strike cancelled out Mary McAteer's early finish for the Black Cats, to secure Darren Carter's side a point at St. Andrew's.

Blues' unbeaten league run was extended to three games with a scintillating 4-0 thrashing of Sheffield United at Bramall Lane. Gemma Lawley headed in from a corner a minute into the match before a wonderful strike from Martha Harris made it two at the break. Second-half goals from Lucy Quinn and Remi Allen completed the scoring for Birmingham.

Carter's side made it back-to-back wins with a dominant 5-2 victory over Watford. Ivana Fuso opened the scoring, with Lily Agg adding a second from the spot and Charlie Devlin finishing from close range for number three. The Hornets got one back early in the second half, but Blues extended their lead with efforts from Smith and Ellie Mason before Lucia Leon added a late second for Watford.

Lucy Quinn's performances for Blues during October won her the Barclays Women's Championship Player of the Month award, and teammate Gemma Lawley picked up the prize for November too as Birmingham continued their winning streak.

Reading were defeated 2-1 at St. Andrew's thanks to a brace from Devlin, before Lawley netted her second of the season in a 1-0 triumph over 10-player London City Lionesses.

Blues made it five wins on the bounce with a 3-1 defeat of Durham. Jade Pennock netted her first goal of the season, Fuso struck from 12 yards out for Blues' second and though Durham pulled one back, a second-half header from substitute Allen secured all three points for Birmingham.

A 3-0 victory over Sunderland saw Carter's side move to the top of the Championship table heading into the Christmas break. A Goal of the Month-winning strike from Agg, on her 30th birthday, set Blues on their way before a Brianna Westrup own goal doubled their advantage and Jade Moore netted their third.

A superb strike from Cho So-hyun proved the difference as Blues completed a league double over London City Lionesses in their first Championship game of 2024, before their winning league run finally came to an end against Watford (0-2). A further defeat against Southampton (1-2), where Blues had led after five minutes through Fuso, was followed by a goalless draw with Blackburn in B9.

Birmingham returned to winning ways in style… with six goals in their next two games. They put four past Reading with no reply under the lights at the Select Car Leasing Stadium. Moore opened the scoring against her former club before Smith netted her sixth goal of the season and Agg completed the rout with a brace in the second half.

Lewes were then defeated 2-0 thanks to strikes from Devlin and Walker.

After back-to-back defeats against Charlton (1-3) - where Lucy Quinn converted from the penalty spot for Blues' goal - and Crystal Palace (0-1), Birmingham completed another season double against Sheffield United, beating them 1-0 in their final home game of the season. In what was Amy Merricks' first game in charge after Darren Carter's departure, Agg scored her sixth goal of the campaign to secure all three points in front of a record crowd of 3,101 at St. Andrew's.

Despite hitting the woodwork twice, Blues' final game of the season ended in a 1-0 defeat at Durham.

Blues' FA Women's Continental League Cup campaign began with a 3-0 defeat to Women's Super League side Brighton & Hove Albion in Group E.

They were also beaten 1-0 by Charlton Athletic, but a header from Lily Agg and a superb volley from Martha Harris gave Blues a 2-1 win over West Ham United – who're also in the WSL – in their final group game. Sadly, it wasn't enough to see them progress to the knockout phase.

Goals from Choe Yu-ri and Ivana Fuso gave Blues a 2-0 victory over Milton Keynes Dons as they entered the Adobe Women's FA Cup at the third-round stage. Darren Carter's side left it late, with both strikes against the National League South outfit coming in second-half stoppage time.

Blues travelled to Burnley in the fourth round where they dominated the game and went ahead through Libby Smith on 21 minutes. It was looking like that would be enough for Birmingham to clinch victory, but Dons equalised from the penalty spot in the 95th minute, forcing extra time. Claudia Walker put Blues back in front before Jade Moore made it 3-1 at the final whistle.

Carter's side found themselves in the lead after just two minutes of their fifth-round tie against WSL side Leicester City, as the Foxes' Deearna Goodwin put through her own net. Leicester scored two quick goals to go in front after 23 minutes, but Smith pulled Blues level shortly before half-time. Unfortunately, the Foxes netted a further four times as Blues bowed out of the competition.

# CROSSWORD

## AKA — ALSO KNOWN AS!

**Fill in the nicknames of Blues' League One opponents!**

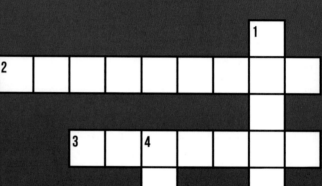

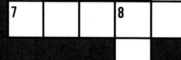

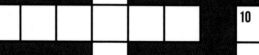

### DOWN

1. Barnsley (5)
4. Reading (6)
5. Lincoln City (4)
8. Exeter City (8)
10. Stevenage (4)

### ACROSS

2. Wycombe Wanderers (9)
3. Bristol Rovers (7)
6. Stockport County (7)
7. Mansfield Town (5)
9. Shrewsbury Town (6)
11. Rotherham United (7)
12. Peterborough United (4)

Solution on page 60.

# WORDSEARCH

| | | | | | | | | | | | | | | | | | | |
|---|---|---|---|---|---|---|---|---|---|---|---|---|---|---|---|---|---|---|
| B | A | N | S | V | X | S | Y | F | S | J | O | S | H | H | L | Q | R | T | E |
| M | B | W | F | W | Y | D | N | N | P | S | H | G | D | R | P | B | B | H | M |
| F | A | R | K | H | L | V | R | I | D | F | R | I | H | T | N | B | J | Q | N |
| Z | T | Q | Z | R | L | F | J | M | N | J | D | Z | G | I | I | T | C | M | A |
| F | B | I | U | B | N | T | T | U | M | C | L | E | C | R | L | G | X | L | D |
| T | O | F | Z | M | W | O | Q | U | N | L | E | V | T | P | T | F | L | Q | V |
| A | C | Q | K | V | S | C | Y | O | O | X | I | J | V | K | O | S | A | H | U |
| N | R | G | X | D | F | H | S | Q | F | A | F | F | W | G | O | L | O | J | M |
| D | G | N | A | H | C | T | D | G | Z | S | S | D | T | P | K | Q | K | D | A |
| B | W | W | O | X | V | Z | V | I | K | M | N | B | M | F | S | K | T | K | L |
| M | N | K | R | N | B | S | K | P | B | S | A | R | U | Y | B | I | P | T | L |
| T | V | P | N | F | I | Z | N | X | Q | J | T | Z | H | A | L | L | L | F | C |
| I | A | W | D | V | E | S | H | B | R | H | S | J | L | M | A | E | R | M | U |
| P | J | P | G | B | X | B | H | F | W | X | H | U | C | I | Q | I | U | O | O |
| G | G | I | P | P | C | V | Y | T | M | D | T | W | R | I | V | B | E | C | Z |
| C | E | G | X | T | K | G | Z | F | K | W | E | D | M | M | U | O | W | C | U |
| R | E | R | A | L | K | V | J | T | W | I | L | G | F | J | Q | W | G | H | V |
| W | Q | M | K | A | A | F | B | A | F | N | I | N | G | J | Q | B | M | S | T |
| D | Z | R | A | K | P | W | G | N | A | N | A | N | A | H | C | U | B | Q | Q |
| E | S | M | W | K | G | N | R | X | Q | X | E | E | S | F | W | E | W | H | I |

**Can you find the surnames of seven Blues Men's first teamers?**

| | |
|---|---|
| ALLSOP | STANSFIELD |
| BIELIK | KLARER |
| BUCHANAN | LAIRD |
| CHANG | |

Solution on page 60.

# ST. ANDREW'S IMPROVEMENTS

**Blues invested £15m in the summer of 2024, making improvements at St. Andrew's @ Knighthead Park and its two training grounds.**

A bulk of that money paid for two fan parks at St. Andrew's – a pop-up one outside the Kop and a permanent one in the Main Stand car park behind the Royal George, which can hold more than 1,000 people on a matchday and houses a kids play area, five-a-side and teqball as well as a food, bar and stage area.

Two giant LED screens were installed on the Kop and Gil Merrick Stands while Wi-Fi was installed for fan use and the Tannoy system inside the stadium has been upgraded too.

At the training grounds, Blues Women now have access to facilities of an elite standard at Knighthead Performance Centre, with a newly refurbished changing area and gym, and a brand-new hybrid training pitch. At the Men's training ground (EPIC) in Henley-in-Arden, the quality of the warm up area has been improved.

# BLUES NEW

Birmingham City's plans for a new stadium have taken a step forward, with the Club's owners purchasing a 48-acre site in East Birmingham.

Knighthead's ambition is to create a Sports Quarter on the former Wheels motor-racing site in Bordesley Park, which would be home to a world-class stadium and training facilities for all Blues teams, as well as extensive commercial and community facilities.

Once operational, the development is expected to generate over 3,000 local jobs.

# STADIUM

Knighthead Co-CEO and Chairman, Tom Wagner, said:

"When we invested in Birmingham City, we made it very clear that we had an ambitious vision to transform the experience for our fans and make a positive contribution to the growth and vitality of the city of Birmingham. The acquisition of the former Wheels site is an important next step in making this a reality.

"The plans for the Sports Quarter will bring global interest to our Club and to Birmingham as a whole. It is going to transform the future of our Men's, Women's and Academy teams, and the fortunes of the community that we call home. We are excited to collaborate with the fans, the local community, and key partners in Birmingham to deliver on our plans for the Sports Quarter."

# BACK IN ACTION!

On Monday 1 July 2024, the Men's first team returned to the Birmingham City Elite Performance and Innovation Centre as preparations ramped up for the 2024/25 Sky Bet League One campaign.

The squad reported in the morning for initial observations before conducting several tests in the gym with the support of staff from the Physical Performance Department and Medical Department.

In the afternoon, joined by a selection of Under-21s players, the group took to the pitch for a session led for the first time by Manager, Chris Davies, and directly supported by Assistant Manager, Ben Petty.

# 2024/25 PRE-SEASON ROUND-UP

## PADERBORN 07 5-0 BLUES

Blues travelled to Austria for pre-season training in July 2024, where they played their first friendly match of the summer, against Paderborn 07. It was a tough game for Chris Davies' side at Pendlingstadion as the new Birmingham City boss named a line-up mixed with youth and experience. New signings Alfie May, Bailey Peacock-Farrell, Ryan Allsop and Emil Hansson made their debuts for the Club, and though Blues had chances, they couldn't find the target.

## SOLIHULL MOORS 0-3 BLUES

Blues beat fellow West Midlanders Solihull Moors to retain the Arthur Cup – a match, which raised funds for the NSPCC and Moors Foundation in memory of six-year-old Arthur Labinjo-Hughes who tragically died in June 2020. May, Kōji Miyoshi, and substitute Lukas Jutkiewicz netted at the ARMCO Arena as Davies secured his first win as Blues boss.

## SHREWSBURY TOWN 0-2 BLUES

Birmingham City secured back-to-back wins with a 2-0 victory over League One Shrewsbury Town. Alex Cochrane and Allsop made their first starts in blue along with Willum Willumsson, who came straight into the side a day after signing for the Club. Jordan James got the opener inside 20 minutes when he rifled the ball into the far corner at the second attempt and Jutkiewicz made sure of victory when he tapped home a cross from Romelle Donovan with just over five minutes remaining.

## BLUES 2-1 RANGERS

Blues beat Rangers 2-1 in the Trevor Francis Memorial Match. Kick-off at St. Andrew's @ Knighthead Park was preceded by a minute of applause in honour of Birmingham City's greatest-ever player, who also represented the Gers during the 1986/87 season. An own-goal from Rangers' James Tavernier opened the scoring for Blues after 10 minutes and May doubled the advantage nine minutes before the break. Scott Wright did pull one back for the Light Blues during the second half, but Davies' men held on for the win.

## WALSALL 0-1 BLUES

Alfie May's 60th-minute goal, his third since arriving from Charlton Athletic, was the difference at the Poundland Bescot Stadium as Blues made it five wins in five in pre-season. He almost had another just moments later, combining with Siriki Dembélé, but his low, curling shot hit the post.

## ALDERSHOT TOWN 3-1 BLUES

Whilst one XI faced Walsall in the Midlands, another Blues team lined up at the EBB Stadium to take on Aldershot. Keshi Anderson put the visitors in front in the seventh minute when he hammered home a delightful ball from Hansson. Shots captain Ryan Jones equalised with a half-volley and they extended their lead just moments later. Both Jutkiewicz and Tyler Roberts were denied by the woodwork as Blues went in search of a leveller but it was the hosts who found the net against the run of play to make it 3-1 at the final whistle.

## BLUES 4-1 WEST BROMWICH ALBION

Blues wrapped up their pre-season preparations with a comprehensive 4-1 home victory over local rivals West Bromwich Albion. May got Blues' first on 20 minutes before Kyle Bartley equalised for the visitors to make it 1-1 at the break. Birmingham increased the pressure in the second 45 and new recruit Christoph Klarer put them in front before Willumsson got Blues' third and May bagged a brace to round off their rout and continue his impressive goalscoring form.

# BCFC AWARDS 2024

**Forward Jay Stansfield picked up all five Men's awards at the BCFC Awards 2024 – a feat never done before – as he was recognised, by both Bluenoses and his teammates, for an outstanding season on loan from Fulham.**

The England Under-21s international scored 12 Championship goals for Blues during 2023/24 which deservedly earnt him the following prizes:

- Supporters' Player of the Season
- Players' Player of the Season
- Young Player of the Season
- Top Goalscorer
- Goal of the Season, for his 96th-minute winner against Plymouth Argyle in August 2023

Speaking to BluesTV after winning his record haul, Jay paid tribute to the fans and his teammates; "I'm really proud. I couldn't do it without the supporters and without my teammates. The fans have been excellent all season, giving not just me encouragement, but the whole team, to stick together and keep going.

"And then for my teammates, I go in every day with them and spend every day with them. And I've made some really good friends here."

NEVE HERRON

Neve Herron, who joined Blues Women in the summer of 2023, collected two awards as the defender was recognised by her teammates with the Women's Players' Player of the Season award and also the Women's Young Player of the Season award.

Midfielder Lily Agg also picked up two awards. She was selected by Bluenoses as the Supporters' Women's Player of the Season after an impressive debut campaign, and also won the Women's Top Goalscorer award, joint with Libby Smith, with six strikes each.

LILY AGG

LILY AGG & LIBBY SMITH

The Women's Goal of the Season prize went to Martha Harris, for her long-range effort against Sheffield United in October 2023.

MARTHA HARRIS

# DRUMMING THE BLUES BEAT!

## UB40 drummer Jimmy Brown reflects on his lifelong love affair with Birmingham City Football Club...

**Q** Hi Jimmy. First of all, can you tell us how you became a Birmingham City supporter?

**A** I was born in Small Heath, and I lived about half a mile from the ground. My dad used to take me on a Saturday. I was a regular for quite a while, but I don't go so often anymore. You don't really choose the team. The team chooses you. And when you've got the connection with a team, that's cemented for life. I've been a Bluenose ever since.

**Q** What are your earliest Birmingham City memories?

**A** I started going to St. Andrew's in the 1960s. We had a pretty decent Birmingham team around that time. More than the football, I remember the sights, the noises even the smells around going to the match.

**Q** What have been your highlights supporting Birmingham City over the years and why?

**A** The most exciting time for me following Blues was when Alex McLeish and then Chris Hughton were managers (from 2007 to 2012). That was a fantastic time, winning promotion to the Premier League (in 2009) and winning the League Cup (in 2011). We had a really good team with Joe Hart in goal and then Ben Foster after that. I really liked the big chap up front, Nikola Žigić, and Sebastian Larsson was a brilliant player too.

Going way back, every Birmingham City fan fortunate enough to watch Trevor Francis will have fond memories of him in a Blues shirt and I'm no different! There were periods around then when we were really competitive and a joy to watch.

Jude Bellingham is another name I have to mention. I love watching the internationals and seeing him in the Euros, playing the way he does - getting the ball and making something happen with it – it's incredible. He's the kind of player any team would want. He's young and fearless.

**Q** Were you at Wembley for the League Cup Final triumph over Arsenal in 2011?

**A** I wasn't, as we were travelling as a band at the time. I think we might have been in Switzerland or maybe in Sweden. We managed to get the match up on the TV in the waiting area (in an airport) and Blues went ahead first but Arsenal

equalised soon after. Then we had to get on
the plane. One of the guys is an Arsenal fan.
We got the message on the plane that we'd
won. A big cheer went up in the plane and
people were wondering what was going on!
There were 10 or 11 of us travelling and it
was mayhem as there were lots of Bluenoses!

**Q** How incredible was it playing a UB40 gig at St. Andrew's last season? How did that opportunity come about?

**A** It was the idea of our management, who had got to meet the new ownership at the Club. We got introduced through Steven Knight, who wrote Peaky Blinders. Around that period, I was starting to go to matches more regularly again, with the Club very kindly giving us pretty much an open invite for matches. Eventually, we discussed the idea of a gig at St. Andrew's and agreed to do it.

I worried that maybe we'd been a bit ambitious as there was the potential for things to go wrong, particularly if Blues lost and we were obviously on after the match. But luckily, everything came together on the day. Blues won and the sun came out. We had a brilliant time. We were really, really chuffed we'd got to do it. It was something great for the Club to offer. They invested money into that show and provided it free for the fans. And I think that the fans really appreciated it.

We might do it again in the future. We'll see what happens.

**Q** Despite the disappointment of last season, how hopeful are you of an instant return to the Championship for Blues in 2024/25?

**A** Obviously, nobody wanted the relegation to happen but there's optimism here because you sense the commitment from the Club that relegation is not going to change the trajectory of the Club. It sounds strange to say, because we've been relegated, but we actually feel like we're moving forward as a Club. There are exciting times ahead, with the new stadium etc. I'm very confident we'll get promoted this season and the relegation will mean we'll just need to work a little bit harder and wait a little bit longer to reach the top-flight, which is what everyone is aiming for. I'll be coming to plenty of games, I'm sure.

MYTH & JONES

**Q** Who were your standout performers for Blues in 2023/24? Despite it being a difficult season, what happy memories do you have of the campaign?

**A** Jay Stansfield had a fantastic season on loan from Fulham, getting the number of goals he did. I thought Kōji Miyoshi did really well. I'm hoping he'll still be with Blues when this Annual goes to press as I think he'll be able to do big things for us in League One.

**Q** For younger readers, can you tell us a bit about UB40 and your history?

**A** We've been going a long time - we celebrated our 45th year in 2024. We released an album called UB45 in 2024 that was in the top five in the UK charts. We released a special CD version of that with the Birmingham City crest on and we did a recording of Forever True with some of the players from the Men's and Women's teams.

In terms of UB40, we're just a bunch of lads from inner city Birmingham who dreamed of being in a reggae band. We became the biggest reggae band in the world. So, it's a real sort of rags to riches story!

**Q** Which other UB40 members support Blues? And are there supporters of other clubs in your ranks?

**A** Myself and Earl (Falconer) are the biggest Blues supporters in the band. We fly the flag for Birmingham City. We're both Small Heath lads.

Brian (Travers), who is sadly no longer with us, invented that sax line that Blues fans sing when they score. The irony is Brian was a Villan, not a Bluenose. But he was just happy the song was embraced, even if it was by a rival Club. You can't buy that sort of cultural reference.

**Q** What does 2025 have in store for UB40?

**A** We've signed up with a big agency. We're hoping for big gigs going forward, Glastonbury, that kind of thing. The next few years are going to be really good for the band, on the back of our album release in 2024 and doing an extensive tour. We're looking forward to it!

**You can follow UB40 on Instagram - @ub40official**

# BLUES SUPER QUIZ

1. What were Birmingham City known as when they were founded in 1875?

2. By what full name is St. Andrew's currently known?
A) St. Andrew's @ Bullring Park, B) St. Andrew's @ Knighthead Park or C) St. Andrew's @ Cannon Hill Park

3. Which Blues legend became English football's first £1m footballer when he moved to Nottingham Forest in 1979?

4. Which national team do both Cho So-hyun and Choe Yu-ri play for?

5. Which Championship club did Ryan Allsop play for prior to signing for Blues in the summer of 2024?

6. Who was Blues manager when the Club won the Football League Cup in 2011?

7. How many seasons have Birmingham City played in the top-flight of English league football to date? A) 40, B) 50 or C) 57

8. Birmingham City Women finished as runners-up in the inaugural FA Women's Super League in 2011… True or False?

9. Which reggae band played a concert at St. Andrew's after Blues' 1-0 win over Preston North End on Easter Monday 2024?

10. Who was Blues Men's top goalscorer in 2023/24, with 13 goals in all competitions?

11. Lily Agg and which other forward was Blues Women's top goalscorer in 2023/24?

12. At which Premier League club was Chris Davies senior assistant coach under Ange Postecoglou prior to his appointment as Blues Men's first team Manager in June 2024?

13. Blues Men's final League One fixture of the season will be played at the Abbey Stadium, which is home to which club?

14. What is the name of Blues' shirt sponsor for the 2024/25 season?

15. In which showpiece fixture were Blues beaten 3-1 by Manchester City on 5 May 1956?

**16** Which Finnish striker scored 17 Premier League goals in 2003/04 to help Blues to a top-half finish in the division?

**17** Which Scottish Premiership club were Blues' opponents for a pre-season friendly in July 2024?

**18** The name of which touchline stand at St. Andrew's is shared with a large, goal end stand at Liverpool's Anfield stadium?

**19** Which manager guided Blues to their highest league position – sixth in the old First Division – in 1955/56?

**20** Which international competition did Blues legend Christophe Dugarry win with France in 1998?

**21** From which country are Paderborn 07, who Blues faced in pre-season in the summer of 2024?

**22** Which seven-time NFL Super Bowl-winner owns a minority stake in Birmingham City?

**23** During the 2024/25 season, Blues will face which Welsh club in the league for the first time since 1994/95?

**24** With 267 goals in 445 appearances between 1920 and 1935, who is Blues Men's all-time leading goalscorer?

**25** Which fellow West Midlands team were Blues' opponents in the 1931 FA Cup Final?

**26** Who scored Blues' winning goal in the 1995 Football League Trophy Final?

**27** As of the end of the 2023/24 season, how many times have Blues Women won the Women's FA Cup?

**28** Which other West Midlands club was Blues defender Layla Banaras eligible to play for during the 2023/24 season?

**29** What is Blues' former Coventry Road ground also known as…? A) Muntz Street, B) Simpsons Street or C) Flanders Street

**30** Who wrote the song 'Keep Right On To The End Of The Road' in 1924, which has since been adopted as Blues' anthem?

# ANSWERS

## CROSSWORD

2. CHAIRBOYS
1. TYKES
3. PIRATES
4. ROYALS
5. IMPS
6. HATTERS
7. STAGS
8. GRECIAN
9. SHREWS
10. BORO
11. MILLERS
12. POSH

## WORDSEARCH

| | | | | | | | | | | | | | | | | | | | | |
|---|---|---|---|---|---|---|---|---|---|---|---|---|---|---|---|---|---|---|---|---|
| B | A | N | S | V | X | S | Y | F | S | J | O | S | H | H | L | Q | R | T | E |
| M | B | W | F | W | Y | D | N | N | P | S | H | G | D | R | P | B | B | H | M |
| F | A | R | K | H | L | V | R | I | D | F | R | I | H | T | N | B | J | Q | N |
| Z | T | Q | Z | R | L | F | J | M | N | J | D | Z | G | I | I | T | C | M | A |
| F | B | I | U | B | N | T | T | U | M | C | L | E | C | R | L | G | X | L | D |
| T | O | F | Z | M | W | O | Q | U | N | L | E | V | T | P | T | F | L | Q | V |
| A | C | Q | K | V | S | C | Y | O | O | X | I | J | V | K | O | S | A | H | U |
| N | R | G | X | D | F | H | S | Q | F | A | F | F | W | G | O | L | O | J | M |
| D | G | N | A | H | C | T | D | G | Z | S | S | D | T | P | K | Q | K | D | A |
| B | W | W | O | X | V | Z | V | I | K | M | N | B | M | F | S | K | T | K | L |
| M | N | K | R | N | B | S | K | P | B | S | A | R | U | Y | B | I | P | T | L |
| T | V | P | N | F | I | Z | N | X | Q | J | T | Z | H | A | L | L | L | F | C |
| I | A | W | D | V | E | S | H | B | R | H | S | J | L | M | A | E | R | M | U |
| P | J | P | G | B | X | B | H | F | W | X | H | U | C | I | Q | I | U | O | D |
| G | G | I | P | P | C | V | Y | T | M | D | T | W | R | I | V | B | E | C | Z |
| C | E | G | X | T | K | G | Z | F | K | W | E | D | M | M | U | O | W | C | U |
| R | E | R | A | L | K | V | J | T | W | I | L | G | F | J | Q | W | G | H | V |
| W | Q | M | K | A | A | F | B | A | F | N | I | N | G | J | Q | B | M | S | T |
| D | Z | R | A | K | P | W | G | N | A | N | A | N | A | H | C | U | B | Q | Q |
| E | S | M | W | K | G | N | R | X | Q | X | E | E | S | F | W | E | W | H | I |

## BLUES SUPER QUIZ

1. SMALL HEATH ALLIANCE
2. (B) ST. ANDREW'S @ KNIGHTHEAD PARK
3. TREVOR FRANCIS
4. SOUTH KOREA
5. HULL CITY
6. ALEX MCLEISH
7. (C) 57
8. TRUE
9. UB40
10. JAY STANSFIELD
11. LIBBY SMITH
12. TOTTENHAM HOTSPUR
13. CAMBRIDGE UNITED
14. UNDEFEATED
15. FA CUP FINAL
16. MIKAEL FORSSELL
17. RANGERS
18. THE KOP
19. ARTHUR TURNER
20. THE FIFA WORLD CUP
21. GERMANY
22. TOM BRADY
23. WREXHAM
24. JOE BRADFORD
25. WEST BROMWICH ALBION
26. PAUL TAIT
27. ONCE – IN 2011/12
28. WOLVERHAMPTON WANDERERS
29. (A) MUNTZ STREET
30. HARRY LAUDER

REBECCA HOLLOWAY

61